TOP 10 STRANGEST ANIMALS

BY BRENNA MALONEY

Children's Press®
An imprint of Scholastic Inc.

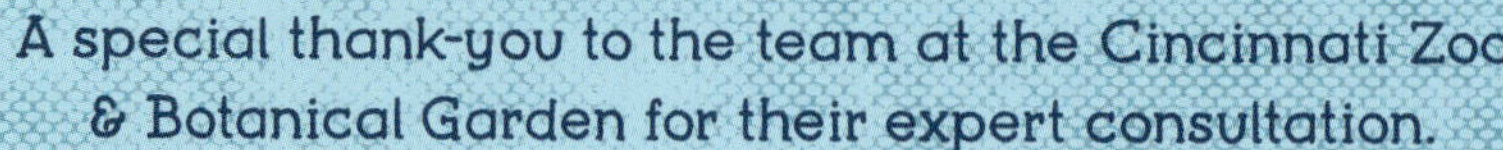
A special thank-you to the team at the Cincinnati Zoo & Botanical Garden for their expert consultation.

Library of Congress Cataloging-in-Publication Data available

ISBN 978-1-5461-3605-7 (library binding)
ISBN 978-1-5461-3606-4 (paperback)

10 9 8 7 6 5 26 27 28 29

Printed in China 62
First edition, 2025

Book design by Kay Petronio

Photos ©: cover, 1: Stephen Dalton/Avalon.red/Alamy Images; 4 center right: Cliff/Flickr; 5 top left: Iva Dimova/Getty Images; 5 top center: Adisha Pramod/Alamy Images; 5 bottom right: AGAMI stock/Getty Images; 7: Wirestock/Getty Images; 10–11 main: Guillermo Ferraris and Mariella Superina; 11 bottom right: Guillermo Ferraris and Mariella Superina; 13 bottom right: Steven Kovacs/Blue Planet Archive; 16–17 main: David Shale/NPL/Minden Pictures; 16 phone: scanrail/Getty Images; 17 bottom right: © 2005 Ifremer/A.Fifis; 19 bottom right: gene1988/Getty Images; 20 bat: shutswis/Getty Images; 23 bottom right: izanbar/Getty Images; 25 bottom right: J. Martin/Northland College/from Anich et al. 2020, Mammalia; 26 main: Claus Lunau/Science Source; 27: Eye of Science/Science Source; 28–29: Eye of Science/Science Source; 30 top right: Steve Gschmeissner/Science Photo Library/Getty Images; 30 bottom left: Michael Arndt/Dreamstime; 30 bottom center: Glenn Bartley/All Canada Photos/Alamy Images. All other photos © Shutterstock.

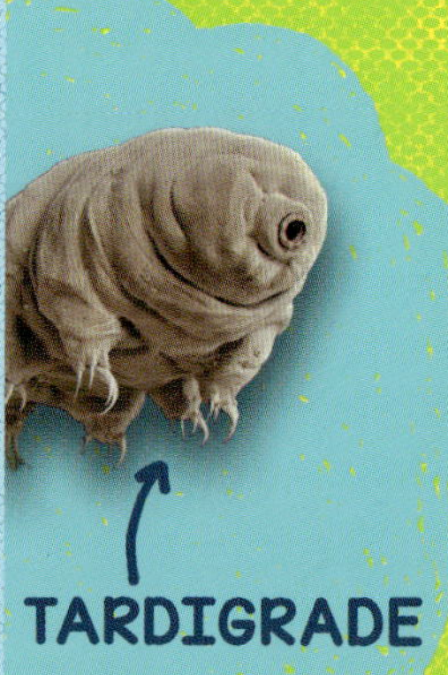

CONTENTS

THE WORLD OF STRANGE

LEAF-NOSED SNAKE

PINK FAIRY ARMADILLO

ORCHID MANTIS

TARSIER

There are so many strange animals in our wild world! Some look odd. Some do weird things. Some eat unusual foods. Some are masters of disguise!

But . . . are you ready to discover which one is the absolute strangest? Read on and count down from ten to one to learn which animal takes the top spot!

A tarsier would win any staring contest. This animal's huge, yellowish eyes look strange. They look even stranger when compared to its small body.

But its big eyes can see well at night. That's when this **nocturnal** creature hunts. A tarsier feeds on insects, **reptiles**, and frogs. It can jump from tree branch to tree branch. And it can snag birds and bats out of the air to eat.

FACT

Tarsiers were named after their long ankle bones called tarsals.

TARSIER CLOSE-UP

FINGERS AND TOES

Extra-long fingers and toes help grasp tree branches. Fingertips have wide, sticky pads.

TARSALS

These long ankle bones help it leap between trees.

LEGS

Its strong back legs can jump 40 times its body length in a single leap!

TAIL

Its scaly tail is twice as long as its body.

EARS

Bat-like ears pick up distant sounds.

EYES

Each of its large eyes weighs as much as the tarsier's brain.

MOUTH

A wide mouth has strong jaws and teeth. This allows the tarsier to eat large prey.

FUR

Soft, grayish-brown fur blends in with trees.

What is pink, furry, *and* has a shell? The very strange pink fairy armadillo! A banded pink shell protects this animal's silky white fur. It protects the armadillo from **predators**.

The shell also helps the armadillo cool down or warm up. This mammal has an underground home. It digs through the sandy soil with large, sharp claws. It hunts for worms and insects to eat.

FACT This armadillo is usually seen alone in the wild.

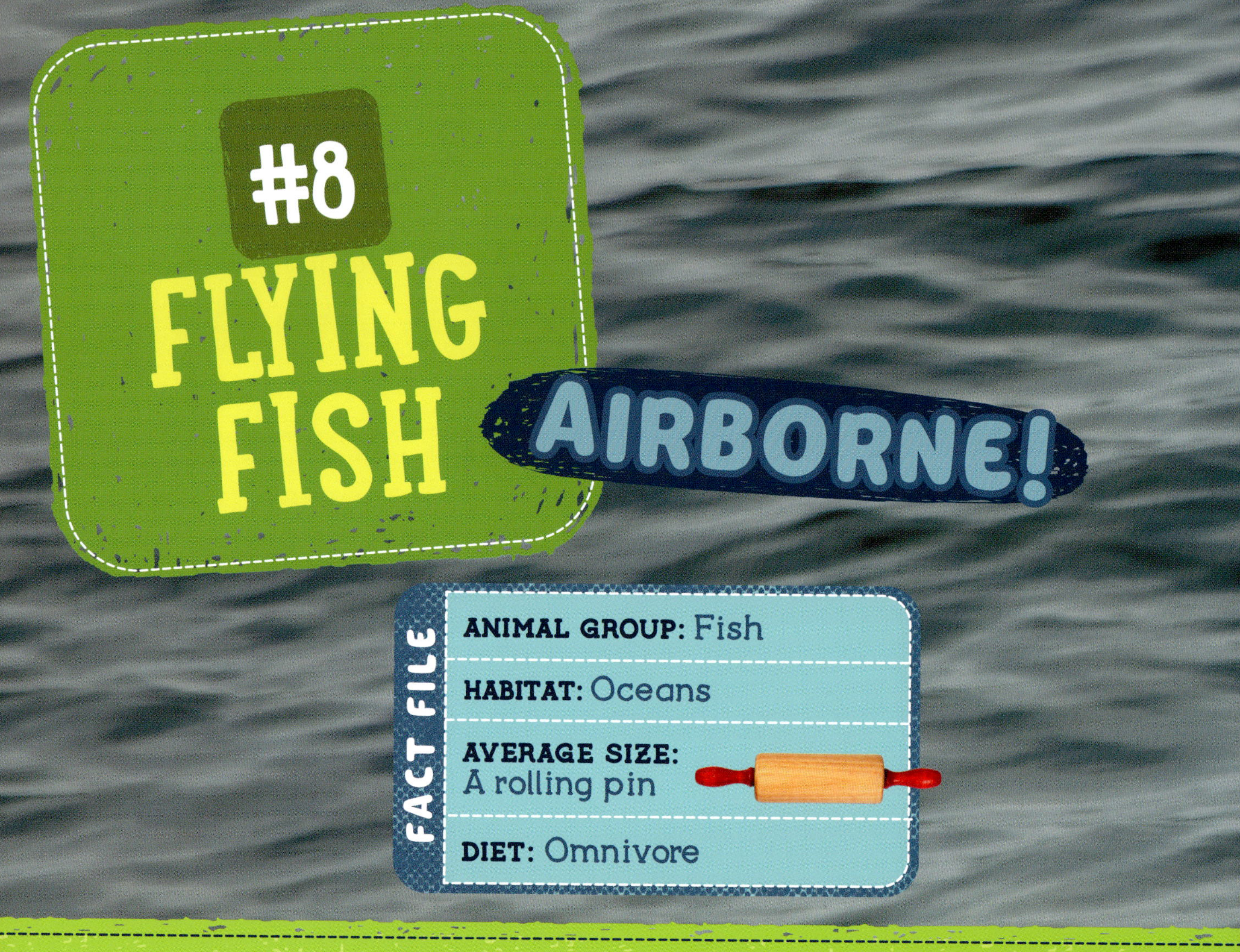

A fish out of water? That's odd! This fish "flies" if it's being chased. It zips through the water at more than 35 miles (56 km) an hour. That is faster than any human can run!

Then, it presses down on its fins and jumps. Once in the air, it glides. A flying fish can glide a distance of almost two football fields in a single jump.

FACT

These fish can "fly" for up to 45 seconds.

#7 POTOO (POH-too)

HIDDEN!

FACT FILE

ANIMAL GROUP: Bird

HABITAT: Forests

AVERAGE SIZE: A banana

DIET: Carnivore

If you're looking for a potoo, you might miss it! This bird sits on top of dead tree branches. It closes its huge yellow eyes. It points its beak upward.

Its feathers blend in. This **camouflage** looks like part of the tree. The potoo stays still until nighttime. Then it hunts. Its big eyes spot prey in the dark. Its wide mouth scoops up flying insects.

FACT

This bird's eyelids allow it to see movement even when its eyes are closed.

Talk about strange animals! Look no further than the hairy, eyeless yeti crab. It lives at the bottom of the ocean. There, it is cold and dark. Tiny openings on the ocean floor release heat.

It's too hot for most animals, but not for this one. The yeti crab waves its arms over these warm places. The heat helps **bacteria** live and grow in its hair. Then the crab eats the bacteria!

FACT

This crab is named after the "yeti"—a mythical snow creature with lots of fur.

#5 STEALTHY!

ORCHID MANTIS

FACT FILE

ANIMAL GROUP: Invertebrate

HABITAT: Tropical rainforests

AVERAGE SIZE: A golf tee

DIET: Insectivore

The orchid mantis may look like a flower. But its bite stings like a bee! This strange pink-and-white insect has petal-shaped legs. Its body sways like it is being blown in the wind.

Its camouflage and behavior trick predators and prey. If another insect gets too close, the mantis stabs it with spiked legs. After it is pinned down, the mantis eats the insect.

FACT

An orchid mantis can change its color. The colors range from light pink to brown.

#4 LEAF-NOSED SNAKE

SLITHERY!

FACT FILE

ANIMAL GROUP: Reptile

HABITAT: Rainforests

AVERAGE SIZE: A baseball bat

DIET: Carnivore

The leaf-nosed snake is something of a mystery. It has a strange nose. Some say it looks like a leaf. But scientists don't know why! This **venomous** snake dangles its nose upside down from tree branches.

Male
leaf-nosed snake

Its scaly skin blends in with the trees. This camouflage makes it look like a vine. The "vine" attracts prey like frogs and lizards.

FACT

Males have noses that are long, narrow, and pointed. Females have broad, flat, and slightly bumpy noses.

Female
leaf-nosed snake

ADORABLE!

#3 AXOLOTL (AK-SUH-LAH-TUHL)

FACT FILE

ANIMAL GROUP: **Amphibian**

HABITAT: Fresh water

AVERAGE SIZE: A lotion bottle

DIET: Carnivore

The axolotl is strange, but really cute! Feathery gills on its head help it breathe underwater. Its mouth is like a vacuum cleaner when hungry.

It sucks up insect eggs and small fish. There's something else that makes an axolotl strange. If injured, it can regrow lost parts of its body! For example, parts of its heart and brain can grow back.

FACT

Axolotls are also known as "Mexican walking fish." That's because they are from Mexico!

There are many reasons why a platypus is strange! It's one of the only mammals that lays eggs. It has a paddle-shaped tail, like a beaver.

A platypus has a sleek, furry body, like an otter. It has webbed feet, like a frog. It has a flat bill, like a duck. A platypus's bill can sense prey. It feeds on insects, worms, and small fish.

FACT

Want more reasons? Under an **ultraviolet light**, a platypus glows blue-green.

#1 TARDIGRADE

INDESTRUCTIBLE!

FACT FILE

ANIMAL GROUP: Invertebrate

HABITAT: Almost anywhere on Earth in water

AVERAGE SIZE: A grain of sand

DIET: Omnivore

The strangest animal lives inside a drop of water. It is a tardigrade! It can only be seen under a microscope. This creature may be the toughest on Earth. A tardigrade can survive almost anything!

Its body has a thin, but strong, outer covering. It can live through being crushed, boiled, or frozen. It can survive being blasted into space. It can last up to 30 years without food or water. Without water, a tardigrade curls up into a dry ball. It rests in this state called a tun.

FACT Tardigrades have been on Earth since before the dinosaurs.

FACT

Tardigrades are also called "water bears" and "moss piglets."

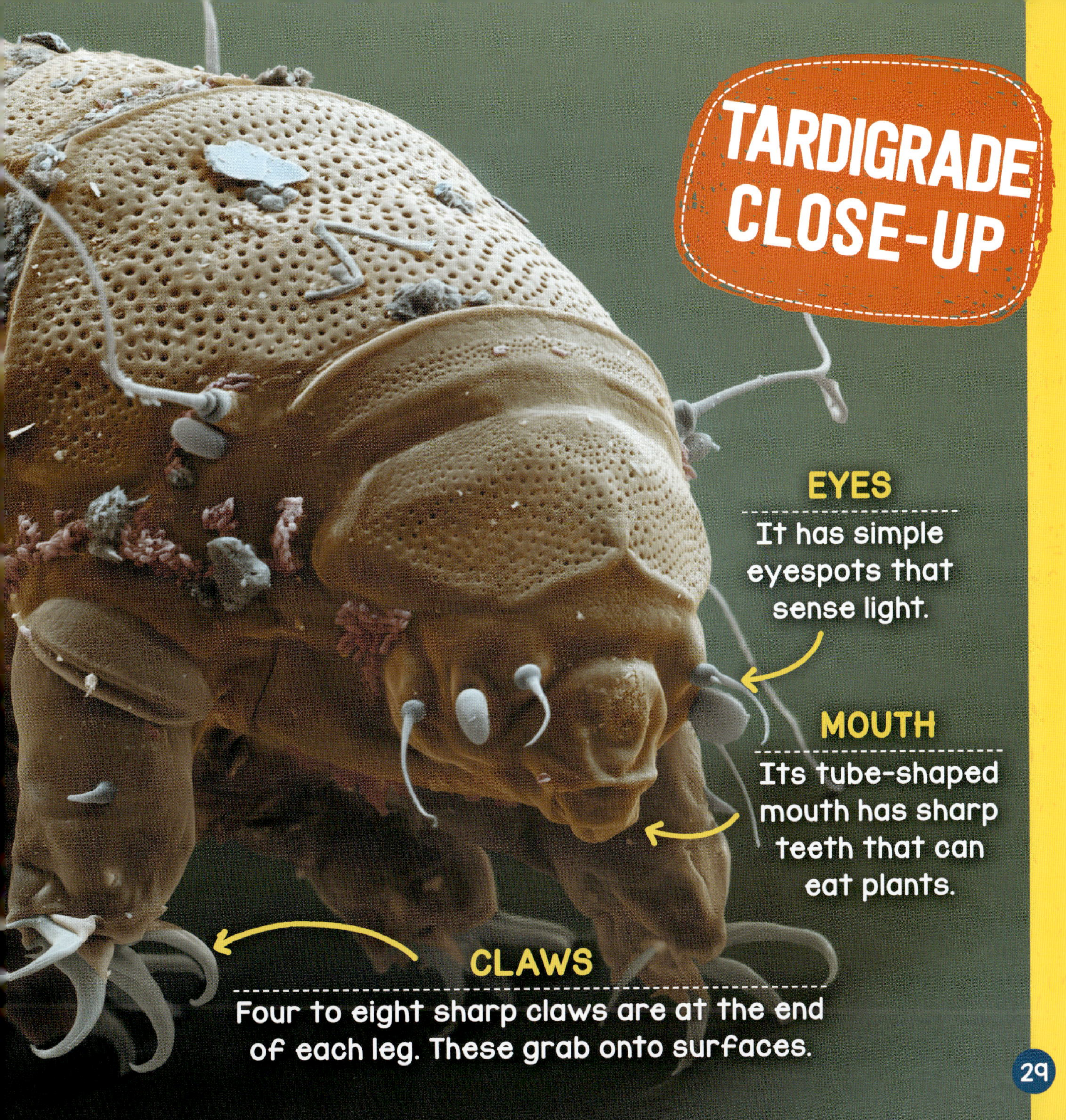
TARDIGRADE CLOSE-UP
EYES
It has simple eyespots that sense light.
MOUTH
Its tube-shaped mouth has sharp teeth that can eat plants.
CLAWS
Four to eight sharp claws are at the end of each leg. These grab onto surfaces.

SIZING THEM UP

There are so many strange animals in our wild world! Some look weird. Some do odd things. Some are hard to explain! Do you agree the tardigrade is the strangest? Or would you pick a different animal? You can probably find even more strange animals and make your own list!